SEPTET

Seven Award Winning Plays from Aotearoa

Edited by June Allen

Kwizzel Publishing

kwizzelnewzealand@gmail.com

PERFORMANCE RIGHTS

Intent to Commit © Kerrie Anne Spicer, 2018 <kerrieaspicer@gmail.com>

Just Looking   © Tim Hambleton, 2018   <jthambleton@xtra.co.nz>

A Star is Born   © Richard Prevett 2018   <playwright.mtm@gmail.com>

The Scarf © Dolly Varden-Chambers 2018 <seldolchambers@xtra.co.nz>

Young Lady in a Boat © Lindsey Brown 2018
<linsadellebrown@gmail.com>

A Colodrama   © Mike Carter 2018   <mikecarter1936@gmail.com>

No Lingering Allowed © Elspeth Tilley 2018 <E.Tilley@massey.ac.nz>

ISBN 978-0-473-46906-1

Edited by June Allen
Cover photo, thanks to Milkovi
Cover design by Bev Robitai

CONTENTS

Intent to Commit   1

Just Looking   11

A Star is Born   23

The Scarf   31

Young Lady in a Boat   39

A Colodrama   49

No Lingering Allowed   55

The plays in this collection were amongst the winning entries in the Playwrights Association of New Zealand short play competition of 2018. It is the third in a series of award winning very short plays which feature other competition winners.

The others are: 'Stage Journeys' edited by Rex McGregor
'Treading the Boards' edited by June Allen

INTENT TO COMMIT

a comedy

by Kerrie Spicer

SYNOPSIS

Two schoolboy would-be gangsters attempt to break into a house to avenge a previous wrong-doing. But do their burglarising skills match their bravado?

CHARACTERS

CASE: 17-year-old wannabe criminal, albeit an intelligent boy of Pacific Island heritage.
RIZZA: 16-year-old accomplice of Case. Fat, occasionally dim-witted white boy who thinks he's black.

SETTING

A low fence runs adjacent to a property. The stage is dimly lit to indicate it is night time.

HAND PROPS

Two torches. Two cans of spray paint. Cigarettes and lighters.

Case and Rizza are looking over the fence, left and right (casing the place). They carry torches and wear black clothes and beanies. Case turns on his torch and shines it through a window of the adjacent property.

CASE: (*To Rizza*) Hey, over there!
Rizza jumps the small fence and peers through the window, illuminated by Case's torch. He looks left to right and then back at Case.

RIZZA: Do you reckon anyone's home?

CASE: Nah, man. There's no cars, no lights. (*Looks behind him*). Even looks like the neighbours are out. We're sweet! This is gonna be easy.
> Case jumps over the small fence just as Rizza turns on his own
> torch, lighting the entire area with its halogen glow.

CASE: What the fuck! Give it here man!
> Case grabs the torch from Rizza and turns it off.

RIZZA: What'd I do?

CASE: You dumb or what? Why don't you just phone the police, tell 'em we're about to burgle 52 Brown Street! Shit, bro. That thing'd light up Eden Park on a sunny day!

RIZZA: Well, you said bring a torch!

CASE: And that's the only one you got? Geez cuz. Really? When your dad works for Lighting Plus?

RIZZA: I never heard any complaints from you when we used it up at Karaka that time.

CASE: When?

RIZZA: That time you nearly shit your pants!

CASE: (*Shaking his head in disbelief*) That was at Spookers, dickhead! To see them ghosts and ghouls before they saw us! We don't want to be seen this time right?

RIZZA: (*Sulking*) Can we just get on with it then?

CASE: (*Looking frustrated*). Okay. Look (*pointing at window*). This one's open a bit. Use your pippies and open it up. Then you jump in and I'll head in after.

RIZZA: Why do I have to go first? I always go first?

CASE: Someone has to go first Rizza and you know what Nike says, so 'just do it'.

RIZZA: What if there's a dog in there?

CASE: Well it'll bark first won't it dickhead! (*He prods him impatiently*). I thought you'd done this before bro?

RIZZA: Yeah, heaps of times.

CASE: Where exactly? School camp?

RIZZA: No time for talking Case, we gotta job to do and you know what Tui said … 'Yeah right.'
    Rizza tries to lift the stiff window with his arms, but it won't budge.
    Case squeezes Rizza's biceps.

CASE: These painted on cuzzie?
    Rizza has had enough and turns and pushes Case with force.

RIZZA: <u>You</u> do it then.
    Case saunters over to the partially open window and tries to open it
    but it won't budge. He looks embarrassed, so flexes his muscles, rolls
    his shoulders back and tries again.

RIZZA: Who's a pussy now?

CASE: I never called you a pussy! That word's just derogatory.

RIZZA: Ooooh, look at you with your fancy schmancy language.

CASE: That's because I actually paid attention at school, Rizza, instead of ogling all the third formers.
RIZZA: Yeah, well. (*Sarcastically*). I'd rather have a nice chick then be able to say 'de de deraga….'

CASE: It's de-rog-a-tory, and this isn't getting us anywhere!

RIZZA: You started it.

CASE: How old are you; five?
    Case turns his torch back on and shines it down the side of the house
    towards the front garden.
CASE (*continues*): I wonder if there's a looser window back there. (*Turns to Rizza*). Can you go check, please?

Rizza starts walking down the side of the house.

CASE: (*Holding his arms out, palms up*). What? No smart-arse remarks?

RIZZA: (*Turning*). You asked nicely.

> *Case continues shining his torch to light Rizza's way. As Rizza gets to the end, he braces himself on the side of the house and peers around the corner mimicking the FBI. He motions the 'all clear thumbs up' at Case and disappears around the side of the house. Case shakes his head and checks the time on his watch.*
> *Case waits. And waits. And waits.*
> *Finally he has had enough waiting and he walks down towards the garden and smashes heads with Rizza who is turning the corner to come back. They both fall over, cursing. Eventually they stand up and dust themselves off.*

CASE: What the hell took you so long?

RIZZA: Well, I went around the side of the house, but it was like, fricken dark! Cos you took my torch off me! So anyway I remembered I had my fags and my lighter in my pocket. So, I lit my lighter so I could see the window … and then I'm just about to peer through the glass when I hear this voice call my name 'Rizza, Rizza'. So I look over to the street and there's Fat Andy! You know the one that shagged your sister.

CASE: (*Incredulously*) Tell me I'm dreaming!

RIZZA: Yeah so, he wanted a light, so I went over and gave him a light and we got talking and yeah, he's good.

CASE: Oh well cuz, that's fucking fantastic (*Rizza nods in agreeance*) I'm really pleased you managed to catch up with him.

RIZZA: Yeah, same.
> *Case slaps Rizza across the face.*

CASE: Witnesses! Rizza! This is meant to be a covert operation. Do you know what <u>covert </u>means?

RIZZA: Here we go again with your big words.

CASE: It's two syllables! And stop changing the subject! Fat Andy is a witness! He can place us here as burglars!

RIZZA: But we haven't take anything?

CASE: But we're <u>gonna</u>!! The only bloody reason we haven't taken anything, dipshit, is because we can't get in! Now, I assigned you the important job of going to find an alternative method of entry and you failed. Miserably!

RIZZA: He needed a light; I had one. That simple.

CASE: You're simple.

RIZZA: Well, that's very deragatary.

CASE: Derogatory! It's very derogatory!
Case and Rizza both lean against the house, frustrated. Rizza pulls out his cigarettes and lights one. He offers one to Case. Case takes it and as he goes to light it, Rizza pulls the lighter away, playfully. Eventually his cigarette is lit and they both lean back and inhale.

CASE: I never knew he shagged my sister.

RIZZA: <u>Everyone</u> knew he shagged your sister.

CASE: Not me. (*Pause*). And she never said.

RIZZA: (*Looking at him incredulously*). Would you really want to have that conversation with her?

CASE: Yeah, nah. (*Pause*). But you should've told me.

RIZZA: Me? Why?

CASE: Cos you're my best mate and I hate his guts.

RIZZA: Really?

CASE: Yeah! He's a piece of shit. I've hated him since …

RIZZA: Nah, I mean … I'm your best mate?
Case looks at Rizza seriously.

CASE: Of course, Rizza! I don't just burgle with everyone.

RIZZA: You currently don't burgle at all!

CASE: Well, that's true.
> *They both have a laugh.*

RIZZA: Why do you want to do this place anyway?

CASE: Well, remember that night we went into town, to that club, and that dickhead bouncer wouldn't let us in.

RIZZA: Which time and which club? They never let us in.

CASE: That time in K'Road a couple of weeks back and that bouncer dude with the afro wouldn't let us in, even though we took those fake ID's.

RIZZA: Your brother's drivers licence?

CASE: Yeah.

RIZZA: Your 40-year-old brother's drivers licence?

CASE: That's beside the point. How was I to know the bouncer could read? Most of them can't.

RIZZA: He could.

CASE: Ok Rizza. On with the story, right! Stop butting in. So, anyway, remember he took my Warriors sweatshirt?

RIZZA: You're here to steal back your Warriors sweatshirt?

CASE: Damn straight!

RIZZA: You brought me here, on this big <u>covert</u> operation, to steal back your Warriors sweatshirt?

CASE: I like it! (*Pause*). It cost me mega bucks. (*Pause*). And anyway cuzzie, you're missing a very pertinent point.
> *Rizza looks confused.*

CASE *(continues)*: That means important.

RIZZA: Well, why don't you just say 'important'?

CASE: The 'pertinent' point I am trying to make is that he shouldn't have taken it, it wasn't his to take and it was wrong, cuzzie!

RIZZA: Yes, Case, it was wrong.
> *Rizza then slaps Case across the face. Case looks shocked, as his hand goes up to his reddened face.*

RIZZA: Frankly, you're lucky I didn't punch you!

CASE: Frankly eh?

RIZZA: Yes, frankly. And anyway. Did you not see that game against the Panthers last week? 36-4! Warriors are playing shit league man. You're probably better off without that sweatshirt. You'd just look like a faggot wearing it.

CASE: What, like your Blues shirt is all that?

RIZZA: Hey! I burnt that two seasons ago. At least I know when to call it quits!

CASE: Pity Tana doesn't.

RIZZA: Hey, he's just the fall guy. He may look like the man, but he doesn't call the shots.

CASE: Yeah, you're right. It's that bozo Bolton.

RIZZA: Yip. He knows as much about rugby as we know about burglarising.

CASE: Burglarising?

RIZZA: Yip.

CASE: Not burglaring?

RIZZA: Nope. Burglarising.

CASE: *(Looking surprised)*. Oh.

RIZZA: I'm not completely thick you know.
> *Case looks a little sad.*

CASE: Actually, Rizza, I don't think you're thick at all. Just … misunderstood.
> *They both finish their cigarettes, stubbing them out on the ground.*
> *Case then bends down and picks up the butts.*

RIZZA: Gross dude. They're finished. I've got more.

CASE: I'm house-cleaning, Rizza. (*He stands up and shows him the butts*). I have one word for you: D.N.A.

RIZZA: That's three.

CASE: Hypothetically yes, but let's not get hung up on numbers. At the end of the day, we could be done for leaving evidence at the scene of a crime. Have you not watched C.S.I?

RIZZA: But we haven't committed a crime.

CASE: True! But not because we didn't want to, and anyway, we shouldn't take any chances. It's good practice.

RIZZA: So. (*Pause*). Whaddya want to do now?

CASE: Admit defeat I guess. (*Looks up at the window*). Damn window! Bloody old houses.

RIZZA: Well, we could still do something.

CASE: Like what?

RIZZA: I dunno. (*Looks around*). Steal his letterbox or something.

CASE: Oooh, so he can't get any post. That's genius!

RIZZA: (*Sarcastically*). Just a suggestion.
> *They both look around, trying to think of a way to avenge the stolen*
> *sweatshirt.*

RIZZA: I've got an idea.

CASE: Shoot.

RIZZA: We do what we do best and leave our mark.

CASE: I didn't bring anything.

RIZZA: I always come prepared, bro.
He pulls out two cans of spray paint and hands one to Case.
RIZZA: As the Chinaman says, 'We spray and walk away.'
They both laugh as the lights dim and we hear the sound of spray paint on weatherboard. Still in the dark ...

CASE: Oh this is good, bro. I feel much better. What'd you write?

The lights turn on and we see Rizza has written on the wall in large, black, gangster-style font "Give back Case's Warriors shirt bro, or he will drop yo' ass."

CASE: RIZZZZAAAAAAAAAA!!!

THE END

JUST LOOKING

A comedy

by Tim Hambleton

SYNOPSIS

A female furniture store salesperson chats to a friend as she waits for a customer. She must urgently make a big sale so tries to start a relationship with a wealthy and vulnerable customer.

CHARACTERS

DEBBIE: 20s or 30s. Furniture store salesperson. Wears store uniform. Dominates her friend. Sexually charged.

ROCHELLE: 20s or 30s. Best friend of Debbie. Wearing a different firm's uniform. Doesn't stick up for herself.

MAN: Mid 40s. Tidy casual dress. Unshaven for a couple of days. A couple of bandages on him.

SETTING

A furniture store.

TIME

Present day.

The two women are sitting on stools chatting in a furniture store.Debbie is working, waiting for a customer; Rochelle is visiting her friend while on a lunch break.

DEBBIE: How long have you got?

ROCHELLE: I don't have to be back till 1.

DEBBIE: Have you got some lunch?

ROCHELLE: Just an apple.

DEBBIE: Is that all?

ROCHELLE: I don't have time in the morning.

DEBBIE: You must have. I mean it's not like you spend a lot of time getting yourself ready.

ROCHELLE: Well I …

DEBBIE: Have you thought about doing something about your eyebrows?

ROCHELLE: You mean a pedicure?

DEBBIE: No; that's your feet.

ROCHELLE: Oh, that'll be why they couldn't help.

DEBBIE: (*Shaking her head*) What's that smell?

ROCHELLE: (*Happy she has noticed*) Oh it's my new perfume. Do you like it?

DEBBIE: (*Blunt*) No. Do you realise flies are dying when they get close to you?

ROCHELLE: No, I didn't.

DEBBIE: Well you can thank me for telling you.

ROCHELLE: (*Despondent*) Thanks.

DEBBIE: No problem. I'll have to go if a customer comes in. I've got to get a sale today; Mr Bruce'll be looking at our end of month stats tomorrow. The highest won't have to do Saturdays for three months! <u>And</u> gets a five hundred buck bonus!

ROCHELLE: How are you going with that?

DEBBIE: That little ferret Simon's just ahead of me – but he's not working today. Some of the others are pretty close though.

ROCHELLE: I could buy something.

DEBBIE: Yeah, right. We've only got quality stuff here, Rochelle.

ROCHELLE: (*Looking a little downcast*) What do you need to sell?

DEBBIE: Something big - like a sofa or a dining table.

ROCHELLE: Mmm. I don't like your chances.

DEBBIE: (*Indignant*) Why not?

ROCHELLE: It's pretty quiet. Oh, no. There are some people down there.

DEBBIE: Yeah. That's Gretchen's end. (*Says "Gretchen" with distain*) She's only been here five minutes - acts like she's my boss.

ROCHELLE: She is your boss, isn't she?

DEBBIE: (*Not wanting to admit it*) Only at the weekends. (*Changing the subject*) As long as we don't get any TWIGs in today.

ROCHELLE: TWIGs?

DEBBIE: Time Wasting Ignorant Gits. They wander around in a day dream and say they're "<u>just looking</u>".

ROCHELLE: Oh, yeah.

DEBBIE: You know some people come in and haven't <u>even</u> got <u>any</u> <u>intention</u> of buying anything.

ROCHELLE: (*Pretending to be surprised*) Really? (*Pause*) You don't ever do that yourself?

DEBBIE: No – I always buy something!

ROCHELLE: Yeah. That does upset Darren a bit, doesn't it.

DEBBIE: Do I look like I care? (*Pause*) Actually 'Chell I've been wanting to talk to you about Darren and me.

ROCHELLE: Have you?

DEBBIE: Yeah. Things aren't great between us at the moment.

ROCHELLE: No?

DEBBIE: No. It's a bit personal aye, but I feel comfortable talking to you about it.

ROCHELLE : Thanks, Debs.

DEBBIE: 'Cos I know you haven't got anyone else to tell.

Rochelle looks downcast but says nothing.

DEBBIE: *(continues)* Things haven't been good for a while. There's a lot of abuse….a lot of put downs.

ROCHELLE: (*Concerned*) I'm sorry to hear that.

DEBBIE: Yeah….but he <u>deserves</u> it. He's such an arse. One thing that does worry me though is the violence.

ROCHELLE: Oh shit, Debs! Are there injuries?

DEBBIE: Yeah – black eyes, bruises, that sort of thing.

ROCHELLE: I've never noticed.

DEBBIE: They're not on me – they're on Darren! I can't stop hitting him!

ROCHELLE: Oh.

DEBBIE: And worst of all – he doesn't know how to please a woman.

ROCHELLE: Oh, Debs.

DEBBIE: He doesn't even know where the ironing board is!

ROCHELLE: Shit; it is bad.

DEBBIE: Tell me about it. And you know his….his…his thing.

ROCHELLE: Yeah.

DEBBIE: It's really starting to come between us.

ROCHELLE: Is it?

DEBBIE: You know how small it is?

ROCHELLE: Yeah. Tiny.

DEBBIE : Miniature. But he's proud of it. He's _always_ playing with it. _And_ he likes to _show it_ to people. I'm always saying _'put it away'_, Darren!

ROCHELLE: I can see why.

DEBBIE: I mean what 30 year old still plays with a train set?!

ROCHELLE: I know. So what are you going to do Debs?

DEBBIE: I would _never_ leave Darren… in February. It's his birthday. But after that….?

ROCHELLE: You've been with him a long time.

DEBBIE: I know….but I think he needs to be replaced.

ROCHELLE: What – like a piece of furniture?

DEBBIE: Well….yeah. I'm looking to upgrade. Darren's idea of a posh meal out is if there's HP sauce on the table as well as tomato sauce.

ROCHELLE: Have you got anyone in mind?

DEBBIE: Not really. I've been on the internet a bit….just looking you know.

ROCHELLE: Yeah. I know. I have all my relationships on line.

DEBBIE: Is that so…is that so they can't see you?

ROCHELLE: (*Shrugging off the insult*) Pretty much. I've been having a bit of phone sex too.

DEBBIE: (*Surprised*) Really? For the same reason?

ROCHELLE: Yeah. But I prefer phone sex to normal sex. It's less sticky. I have had a couple of embarrassing moments though.

DEBBIE: How?

ROCHELLE: I've rung the wrong number.

DEBBIE: Shit.

ROCHELLE: I got a Presbyterian minister once.

DEBBIE: Really?

ROCHELLE: Yeah. He was very understanding.

DEBBIE: (*Nods*) So - getting back to me. I will feel pretty bad about having to let Darren go, when the time comes.

ROCHELLE: Sure. I can see why you would, but I've never liked him.

DEBBIE: (*Indignant*) Pardon!

ROCHELLE: Nothing.

DEBBIE: What's wrong with Darren?

ROCHELLE: Nothing.

DEBBIE: That's not what you said.

ROCHELLE: I…I …I didn't mean….(*Changing the subject*) What's happening down there?

DEBBIE: (*Waves at Gretchen in the distance. Pretending to smile*)
Gretchen's just sold a bookcase. Bitch. I just want someone with a bit of
class. Refined, cultured you know.

ROCHELLE: I've met a guy on line called Todd. He's refined.

DEBBIE: (*Uninterested*) Ah, huh.

ROCHELLE: He shops at New World. He's smart too. He went to
Polytech. And he's got some really clever ideas about how to make money.

DEBBIE: Like what?

ROCHELLE: Gambling.

DEBBIE: I just want a rich, handsome, intelligent, well-hung man who can
last longer than thirty seconds, to sweep me off my feet. Is that too much to
ask?

ROCHELLE: No.

DEBBIE: No, it's not is it?

> At that moment a man walks into the shop. Tall, well dressed in
> casual clothing, but with some stubble and a couple of bandages on him.
> Both women lean over and check out his arse as he walks past.

DEBBIE: Better go. (*To man*) Can I help you?

MAN: Oh. No. I'm just looking thanks.

DEBBIE: (*Glances over to her friend and smirks*) Of course. (*Continuing
to speak regardless, and shamelessly flirting*) These are made in Germany
Imported exclusively by us. Available in Queen, King and Superking.
Height adjustable. Inner sprung, to prevent roll together – although I don't
mind a bit of that myself. *(She smiles. He doesn't react at all, just sort of
nods and wanders off in a different direction. She follows)* Oh, I see you've
spotted our hanging chairs. They're part of our current outdoor furniture
range. They *are* singles but I'd say you could squeeze someone else in
there with you. (*Raises her eyebrows*) Oh, this piece has got 15% off
today. It's an armoire which interestingly is very close to 'amour' – the
French word for love.

MAN: Um, sorry, I don't mean to be rude but my wife and I were in a car accident last night.

DEBBIE: Really?

MAN: Yes. She's on life support.

DEBBIE: Oh!

MAN: I've been at her bedside for fourteen hours. I've just left the hospital for a few minutes to clear my head. I <u>really</u> am just looking.

DEBBIE: Of course I understand. I'll leave you to it. (*Goes back to Rochelle*)

ROCHELLE: So who is he?

DEBBIE: He was in a car accident yesterday. His wife's on life support.

ROCHELLE: (*Shocked*) Oh!

DEBBIE: He is handsome, isn't he? (*They look at each other; Debbie raises her eyebrows*) He looks wealthy.

ROCHELLE: Debs, you're not thinking…? His wife's on life support!

DEBBIE: (*<u>Shrugging</u>*) It could go either way. (*Looking at something in the distance*) Oh; Ben's just sold a sideboard. Shit. He'll be ahead of me now. (*Looking back at the man*) Was he looking this way?

ROCHELLE: I don't think so.

DEBBIE: I think he might have been. You wouldn't know how to read the signals, Rochelle. (*She hurries back over to him. Sidles up to him and casually slips in this question*) What sort of car were you driving when you had the crash?

MAN: (*A little surprised by the question*) It was written off. Ah…it was an Audi (*She nods; looks away from him with a slight smile*) Why?

DEBBIE: (*Delighted to hear it's an expensive car*) An Audi. Oh, no reason. Are you from around here?

MAN: No; Queenstown.

DEBBIE: (*Again trying not to show how happy she is to hear that*) Queenstown.

MAN: Yes.

DEBBIE: What do you do there?

MAN: I'm a Company Director.

DEBBIE: (*Impressed*) Really?

MAN: Yes.

DEBBIE: (*Nearly under her breath but he hears it*) I'm good company.

MAN: Pardon?

DEBBIE : (*Quickly*) Nothing. Can I interest you in this – it's a lovely chest of drawers isn't it – but I don't really know why they call it a chest. It's not a chest at all, is it? (*She thrusts out her chest towards him but tries not to make it too obvious. He walks away and she quickly follows*) Oh, these mirrors are imported from Spain. Gorgeous, aren't they? You can hang them on the wall, on a wardrobe door, or….. on the ceiling – if…that's your thing. (*She raises her eyebrows*) Did I see you looking at our sheepskins rugs?

MAN: No.

DEBBIE: (*Ignoring him*) Ooo, they're heavenly. You just lie back and luxuriate. The feeling against bare skin is to die for.

MAN : (*Ignoring her. He then receives a text*) Oh, There's a text from the hospital. It's Annette's doctor. (*Reads it. Shocked*) Oh! (*Sits down slowly*)

DEBBIE: (*Quietly hopeful; touches her lower left incisor with her small finger*) So, they're going to turn it off are they?

MAN: No – she's made a miraculous recovery.

DEBBIE: (*Unimpressed*) Great. (*Trying to cover up her lack of compassion*) I mean; that's terrific.

MAN: It's fantastic. We're soul mates, she and I. (*Debs gives fake smile*) There'll be a lot of rehabilitation of course.

DEBBIE: Yeah; I imagine there will be.

MAN: (*Scrolling through the text*) It sounds like she won't be able to get about by herself for some months.

DEBBIE: My aunt had to look after her husband for years. It can be <u>very</u> lonely.

MAN: I have an amazing circle of friends. I'll be fine. (*Pause*) Oh, she's not going to be able to feed herself either.

DEBBIE: That'll probably get you down after a while.

MAN: It doesn't matter – I'd do anything for her.

DEBBIE: Still, you'll probably find you need some way to <u>relax</u>.

MAN: I do yoga.

DEBBIE: (*Knocked back again but still trying*) You can't beat a good short burst of physical exercise to deal with stress.

MAN: I go to the gym three times a week.

DEBBIE: (*Still trying*) You'll need someone to keep you company on those <u>long</u> winter nights.

MAN: I have a dog.

DEBBIE: You'll probably want someone to go to the movies with.

MAN: I have a home theatre.

DEBBIE: (*Getting desperate*) You'll need someone to drive you around.

MAN: I have a second car.

DEBBIE: (*Getting more desperate*) You might want someone to cook for you.

MAN: I'll get 'My Food Bag'.

DEBBIE: (*Now resigned to the fact she isn't going to have a relationship with him*) You know what you need?

MAN: What?

DEBBIE: (*Pointing a finger at him*) A new lounge suite.

THE END

A STAR IS BORN

a comedy

by Richard Prevett

SYNOPSIS

Humphrey is launching a new political party and invites a team of 'experts' to a strategy meeting.

CHARACTERS

HUMPHREY: middle-aged businessman
SCARLETT: Public Relations Consultant
ANDROID: young IT expert
LIONEL: Professor of Political Studies
JONQUIL: young Image Advisor

SETTING

The five cast are seated in a semi-circle around a coffee table with water jug and glasses.

HAND PROPS

Handbags for Scarlett and Jonquil, mobile phones for everyone, iPad for Lionel

The five cast are seated in armchairs in a semi-circle around a coffee table. Each person has an iPad and Jonquil and Scarlett have handbags.

HUMPHREY: Welcome to this historic first caucus meeting of a political party yet to be named. Scarlett has agreed to record the minutes so please state your name and qualifications.

SCARLETT: I'll kick off. I'm Scarlett Forrester a Public Relations Consultant with a degree in Human Gullibility.

JONQUIL: You are looking at Jonquil Paradise, Image Advisor. Formerly a director of the Miss Universe Beauty Pageant.

LIONEL: Professor Lionel Dupree, Policies Strategist from the University of Serendipity.

ANDROID: Android. IT Nerd with an IQ of 160.

HUMPHREY: An impressive line-up. And, of course, I'm Humphrey Grump and I want to be Prime Minister of this damaged country of ours and you good people are going to tell me how to reach this goal. First on the agenda. The name of our political party. Suggestions please.

LIONEL: Ordinary citizens look at their voting paper. Labour? Nah – I don't do work. National? Nah – that's a boring radio station isn't it? New Zealand First. Nah – never heard of them. Green Party? Nah – prefer Orange myself.

JONQUIL: How about Beautiful Party?

EVERYONE: Nah!

SCARLETT: Birthday Party?

EVERYONE: Nah!

ANDROID: Something fizzy like Electronic Party.

EVERYONE: Nah!

LIONEL: I would go for something very dignified like the Worthy Party.

EVERYONE: Nah!

HUMPHREY: What do you think about Our Party?

SCARLETT: Possibility. Put it on the short-list.

JONQUIL: What do we see on current advertising media? My food bag, My bank, My spark so ……. We can be My Party!

EVERYONE: My Party!

HUMPHREY: Brilliant, Jonquil. Next on the agenda. My name.

LIONEL: Yes. With all respect I don't think Humphrey Aloysius Grump is a brand name that would indicate your leadership qualities.

SCARLETT: That's right - you need a name that voters can identify with. Whether they be European, Māori, Immigrant, young, old, male, female.

JONQUIL: Change your name by Deed Poll as soon as possible. I changed my birth name from Agatha Funsengarteen to Jonquil Paradise. Made a huge difference to my career enhancement.

LIONEL: How about Richard John Seddon - hugely respected nineteenth century Prime Minister.

EVERYONE: Nah!

ANDROID: Call yourself Michie McCaw – very close to our revered former All Black captain.

EVERYONE: Nah!

SCARLETT: Close to a celebrity name? John Cruise? Ed Shearing? Tim Kardashian?

EVERYONE: Nah!

JONQUIL: Lee – European name, Chinese name. Willie Apiata – Victoria Cross. Sir Edmond Hilary. There it is! Hilary Apiata – hyphen – Lee

HUMPHREY: Hilary Apiata-Lee. I like it.

ANDROID: And Hilary can be the first name of a man or a woman. Women will vote for you.

SCARLETT: Could pick up transgender voters also.

LIONEL: Get that Deed Poll application in tomorrow, Humphrey.

HUMPHREY: Great stuff, team. So - next my appearance. Your department, Jonquil.

JONQUIL: Complete makeover, Humphrey. Hair extensions, hair colour – dark with a touch of distinguished grey, Botox for the wrinkles, nose reconstruction and body enhancements. I would recommend you book in to a clinic for a month.

SCARLETT: Throw in a new diet, exercise program.

LIONEL: You'll need a fashion designer to make sure you wear the right clothes.

JONQUIL: Way to go, Lionel.

HUMPHREY: Right, everybody. Time for a break. Conga!

 Everybody forms a conga line and circulate chanting "MyParty! MyParty!" and then sits down.

ANDROID: First exercise I've had in years.

JONQUIL: *(after retrieving lipstick and mirror from her handbag. Applies lipstick.)* I did go to the gym this morning.

SCARLETT: Now family Humphrey. We'll have to set you up in a new situation that attracts media attention.

LIONEL: Glamorous wife who doesn't speak but just smiles all the time.

SCARLETT: So before you change your name you can get rid of your current partner.

JONQUIL: Then when you have your new name arrange a spectacular wedding to your new trophy wife and grab the front cover of Women's Weekly.

ANDROID: And get her pregnant eight months before the election so she has the baby just before the polling booths open.

HUMPHREY: I'm very fertile.

SCARLETT: Even more with your new diet and exercise regime.

JONQUIL: I'll line up some models who you may find attractive.

HUMPHREY: I look forward to that. Now - communications, Android.

ANDROID: We will set it up so that every electronic device known to mankind will automatically bring up your name, face and MyParty. Facebook, Twitter, Instagram, Yahoo – the lot. You will be number one in terms of name recognition. People vote for names they recognise even if they don't know much about you.

SCARLETT: In a subliminal way we will promote your wisdom, your understanding, your charisma, your experience and, in general, your likeability.

LIONEL: Make no enemies. Offend no one.

ANDROID: Until after the election.

HUMPHREY: OK. Policies, strategy and other big words, Lionel. What's your plan?

LIONEL: These days the voters find it difficult to identify policy differentials. Mainstream parties all tend to be near the centre. Centre left, Centre right. Therefore most people vote from a selfish point of view. You people are voters. What do you complain about?

SCARLETT: Tax, tax, tax. Fifty percent of my hard earned income goes in tax. GST, ACC levies, rates……

ANDROID: The cost of beer and cigarettes.

JONQUIL: The price of petrol.

LIONEL: So there it is. All about money.

JONQUIL: Are you saying that traffic congestion, immigration, hospital waiting lists etc. will not affect how someone votes?

LIONEL: Probably not. Those kind of things have always been there. The voter is mainly interested in what affects their pocket.

HUMPHREY: So we slash income tax, GST, fuel tax, alcohol tax, cigarette tax.

JONQUIL: The working class, small business, and solo mothers will jump for joy and vote for MyParty.

LIONEL: Exactly.

JONQUIL: I think another policy would be for us to contact the six most popular members of parliament in safe seats and tell them that if they join MyParty they will all be cabinet ministers in our government with triple their existing salaries.

SCARLETT: Splendid idea, Jonquil.

ANDROID: But what about us?

HUMPHREY: There is room for us all. Conga time, everyone.

They all join the conga line chanting "Triple Salary, Triple Salary". Humphrey is at the front and after a little shove from Android he falls over. They gather around full of concern.

SCARLETT: You okay, Humphrey?

HUMPHREY: Yes, yes – I'm all right. Must be all the excitement. Just need to go to the bathroom. (*He exits; the others gather in a huddle.*)

LIONEL: Are you thinking what I'm thinking?

SCARLETT: Obvious to me.

ANDROID: If we want to win that's the way to go.

LIONEL: Jonquil, we think you should be the party leader.

SCARLETT: Your ideas have been brilliant. And Humphrey will simply be too much hard work.

LIONEL: Agreed. An attractive intelligent young woman will appeal to the voters. No need for makeovers and coaching.
ANDROID: Much better to have her pregnant rather than Humphrey's trophy wife. I can help you there, Jonquil.

JONQUIL: What? To get pregnant?

ANDROID: I'll do anything to be a cabinet minister on a triple salary.

SCARLETT: Jonquil Paradise – a perfect name for a Prime Minister. Will attract world attention.
JONQUIL: Thank you so much for your support everyone. I happily accept.

EVERYONE: Congratulations!

Humphrey enters.

HUMPHREY: Congratulations for what?

LIONEL: Sit down, Hilary Apiata-Lee. We have some news for you.

THE END.

THE SCARF

A comedy

by Dolly Varden-Chambers

SYNOPSIS

An elderly woman feigns dementia when her new pastime is uncovered.

CHARACTERS

MRS SCOTTISH: An Elderly Woman
HER DAUGHTER: 35/40ish
FEMALE STORE DETECTIVE: any age

SETTING

A sitting room, early afternoon

TIME

The present

When the scene opens Mrs Scottish is seated in an armchair, she must be wearing a distinctive scarf over her shoulders.

NOISES OFF.

DETECTIVE: Good afternoon, Madam. I am a store detective and I have followed an elderly lady here from a store in town. May I speak to the lady please?

DAUGHTER: You must mean my mother...Yes, of course, this way please.

DAUGHTER: This is my Mother.

DETECTIVE: I see. *(takes out notebook)* Name?

MRS SCOTTISH: Meryl Streep or Rene Zelwegger,! I can never decide which one sounds the funniest. *(she laughs)*

DAUGHTER: Mum!

MRS SCOTTISH: Englebert Humperdink, Phoebe Snow, Michael Buble!...that's a funny one...Cumberbatch, somebody Cumberbatch...

DAUGHTER: No. <u>Your</u> name.

MRS SCOTTISH: Mum...it's Mum.

DAUGHTER: It's Amelia Scottish.

DETECTIVE: Is that your real name?

MRS SCOTTISH: People are always asking me that, <u>and </u>where I come from

DAUGHTER: Mum, stop being silly.

MRS SCOTTISH: Sorry, I thought we were playing that funny name game that we play at the Community Centre on Wednesdays, we always enjoy that...we have to think of a name and it has to be a real funny one and we have....

DAUGHTER: *(Interrupting her)* Stop it! We're not playing that game; this lady is a police woman!

MRS SCOTTISH: Are you? You don't look like one; you're not wearing a uniform or a hat.

DETECTIVE: Nonetheless I am a detective...plain clothes.

MRS SCOTTISH: Yes, they are!

DAUGHTER: Mum! Don't be so rude.

MRS SCOTTISH: Oops, manners...sorry, would you like a cup of tea? No trouble to make you one.

DAUGHTER: Mum, she's here on business.

MRS SCOTTISH: Oh dear, what sort of business?

DETECTIVE: I am a Store Detective.

MRS SCOTTISH: Well, they're not hard to find, I shouldn't think they'd need to have a job like that!

DAUGHTER: Mum, she doesn't look for stores...she works for one and watches the customers.

MRS SCOTTISH: That's nice, dear. Why does she do that?

DETECTIVE: Madam, I am here on a very serious matter.

MRS SCOTTISH: There was a show called that.

DAUGHTER: What do you mean? 'Called what?'

MRS SCOTTISH: Madam...my name is madam, that's what they call me...Oh No, it was "Call me Madam"...Ethel Merman...Oh, that's another funny name, it should have been Mermaid with a name like Ethel eh?

DETECTIVE: Can we get to the point please?

DAUGHTER: Yes, of course...I'm sorry she's like this, it's her age you know.

MRS SCOTTISH: Witherspoon...Reece Witherspoon...that's a good one, I'll bet Janet hasn't thought of that one!

DETECTIVE: Madam, it's about the scarf you're wearing.

MRS SCOTTISH: Do you like it? I thought it was rather pretty too.

DETECTIVE: Yes. It's very attractive, but is it _yours_?

MRS SCOTTISH: Must be...I'm wearing it!

DAUGHTER: It's her new one.

MRS SCOTTISH: A lady gave it to me.

DAUGHTER: A lady...which lady was that, dear?

DETECTIVE: You were seen coming out of "Fleur Bijou" wearing this scarf.

MRS SCOTTISH: Was I ?...I don't usually go in there, it's a very expensive shop, but I did today because it was raining and I liked the funny name. I like funny names you know..."Fleur Bijou"...

DETECTIVE: As I have observed Mrs Scottish...now tell me, did you pay for the scarf?

MRS SCOTTISH: It's rude to pay for presents.

DETECTIVE: Not if you're buying them for yourself, Madam.

MRS SCOTTISH: Oh, but I wasn't. This nice lady gave it to me.

DAUGHTER: Mother, I don't understand; tell me what happened.

DETECTIVE: Yes; please do, Madam.

MRS SCOTTISH: Well, I was looking at the scarves and this nice lady came over and said, "Why don't you put it on, it goes so well with your skirt." So I did, and then she said, "It's perfect... made for you..." So I said, "Is it? Thank you, that's very kind of you." And she said, "My pleasure, Madam."

DAUGHTER: Mum! <u>She was a sales lady!</u>

MRS SCOTTISH: Well, she didn't ask me for any money.

DETECTIVE: Mrs Scottish, it is always assumed the items in a shop are for sale...for cash or on a credit card.

MRS SCOTTISH: There wasn't a notice saying that, and I haven't got one of those card things.

DETECTIVE: Is there a price ticket on the scarf?

MRS SCOTTISH: I don't think so, the lady probably took it off. I always do when I give someone a present. It's really embarrassing if you don't and the people find it. There is only a little H; that must be for happy, 'cos it is a happy scarf isn't it?

DETECTIVE: I remember now, "Fleur Bijou" don't use price tickets; they only use codes.

DAUGHTER: (*patiently*) Mum, she didn't give it to you, she was expecting you to buy it.

MRS SCOTTISH: She didn't say that, I thought it was my present...some shops do give you things.

DAUGHTER: Only little promotional samples.

MRS SCOTTISH: Well, this could have been one of those, how do I know?

DETECTIVE: Madam, the point is, you have a scarf which you haven't bought, we call that shop lifting!

MRS SCOTTISH: Don't be silly, I couldn't do that! *(laughing)*

DAUGHTER: That's just a term Mother, we know you couldn't do that ...

DETECTIVE: Mrs Scottish, I am obliged to charge you with theft and possession of stolen goods.

MRS SCOTTISH: I don't understand what you mean...what does she mean?

DAUGHTER: Surely not, Officer...you can see how she is, this is all a total misunderstanding, my Mother wouldn't steal deliberately...what about if we just give it back?

DETECTIVE: Sorry Madam, I can't do that, that's not usual.

DAUGHTER: Well, she's not usual either is she?, you can see that...this is all a sad misunderstanding...can't you take pity on her?

MRS SCOTTISH:(*crying*) Are you taking my present away?

DETECTIVE: Madam, it is not your present...it is stolen goods!

DAUGHTER: Couldn't you just explain to the company what happened?

MRS SCOTTISH: (*Mumbling away to herself*) Stolen?, it's not stolen...the nice lady gave it to me, it was made for me she said...it's my present.

DETECTIVE: I do have to admit suspects don't usually behave this way...I suppose I could contact the office and see what they want to do with her *(takes out her mobile phone and moves away SL and selects a number)*

MRS SCOTTISH:(*clutching her scarf*) What's she going to do with my scarf?

DAUGHTER: It's not yours Mum, we've just told you that.

MRS SCOTTISH: She gave it to me, it's my present.

DETECTIVE:*(on phone)* Dementia...yes I think so, definitely has...thinks it was given to her as a present...yes, very distressed...code H on the label...Oh yes, very genuine...yes Sir, I think that would be an excellent option in the circumstances...yes, of course I will tell her that...thank you, Sir. Yes; I'll fill in all the appropriate paper work when I get back to the office...good day, Sir.

> *Mrs Scottish and her daughter have been watching from a distance, daughter is consoling the Mother and she is still clutching her scarf and crying...Daughter goes over to Detective when she is off the phone.*

DETECTIVE: (*off phone now*) The manager has made a huge and generous decision Madam, he has allowed your mother to keep the scarf this time, as a present from him, but he asks that she does not go into his shop again in the future.

DAUGHTER: Oh, what a relief! That is extremely generous and kind of him. Please thank him for me.

DETECTIVE: I will, but I think you should make sure your Mother doesn't ever go shopping alone in future...this could have been a very nasty. Court case for her you know; Mr Dewberry is a very understanding man. His own mother suffers with dementia, which probably explains why he was so lenient with your mother.

MRS SCOTTISH: Dewberry?...now that's a funny name ...Dewberry.

DAUGHTER: Mother, <u>don't</u>...stop <u>now</u>!...*(to Detective)* I will make sure she doesn't shop alone in future and also make sure she doesn't go into your shop again.

DETECTIVE: Now Mrs Scottish, you can keep the scarf this time, but you must not go into our shop again, do you understand?

MRS SCOTTISH: Oh, I wouldn't Officer; it's too expensive!

DAUGHTER: (*Hurriedly*) Let me see you out officer, and do thank Mr Dewberry. We really do appreciate his kindness.

MRS SCOTTISH: Dewberry?...is that his real name?...that's a funny name!

DAUGHTER: Mother STOP right NOW! (*she sees Detective out and returns inside*)

MRS SCOTTISH: (*now perfectly normal*) He-he-he a new scarf for me! (*she twirls it around her head laughing as she does so*)

DAUGHTER: Mother, I've told you to stop doing this! One of these days you won't be so lucky and will end up in court!

MRS SCOTTISH: Oh, it's just a bit of fun, I love doing it and it makes me laugh. You don't know how boring it is being a nice little old lady all the time! I have to keep the old brain active or I really will get dementia

DAUGHTER: Well, this really has to be the last time. I'm not going to help you anymore. Okay? And. how did you know Mrs Dewberry has dementia? You took a chance that he would be kind to you.

MRS SCOTTISH: Janet told me; they're cousins. Mr Dewberry gives lots of money to dementia collections, so I felt pretty safe.

DAUGHTER: No more, Mum … please. It's too stressful for me.

MRS SCOTTISH: Okay, Grumble bum ….. Oh, that's a funny name …. Grumble bum!

DAUGHTER: MOTHER!

THE END

YOUNG LADY IN A BOAT

a comedy

by Lindsey Brown

SYNOPSIS

A play for two female characters, set in Victorian times. The 1870
painting 'Young Lady in a Boat' by James Tissot was the inspiration.

CHARACTERS

LILLY: A 19 year old unmarried woman from a wealthy Victorian family
VIOLET: Lilly's mother and chief matchmaker
PETER: A voice, offstage only; 3 lines of dialogue.

SETTING

A row boat and water weeds. However, each may be a two dimensional
cut-out supported from behind.

HAND PROPS

A boat's drain plug attached to ribbons.

*A well-dressed young woman is sitting in a row boat - just like in the image
from the 1870's painting 'Young Lady in a Boat', by James Tissot (minus the
dog and the oar). It is late afternoon. The water weeds are behind her to the*

*right. There is a long pause as she just sits there waiting. She then gives up and
starts moving.*

LILLY: Oh, for goodness sake!
> *There is sudden movement from the water weeds and a head pops up,
> revealing Lilly's mother, Violet. The premise is there is another row
> boat hidden behind the weeds that she is hidden in.*
VIOLET: (*hissing*) Lillian Grace Victoria Edwards, sit back down now!

LILLY: But Mother!

VIOLET: Hush. Keep your voice down!

LILLY: (loud whisper)) This is ridiculous!

VIOLET: No, what's ridiculous is you missing the entire London season.

LILLY: How could I attend when I had been bed ridden for three months?

VIOLET: Yes. Bed Ridden. Only my daughter could catch a child's disease at
19.

LILLY: Whooping cough wasn't a barrel of laughs for me either.

VIOLET: Mind your manners, young lady!

LILLY: (*pause*) Sorry, Mother.

VIOLET: Good. Now sit back properly. Remember your posture. Lower the
blanket down so you can see the frills on your dress.

LILLY: But it's getting cold.

VIOLET: Not nearly as cold as the life of a spinster.
> *Lilly reluctantly does as she is told.*

VIOLET: (*continues*) Good girl. Now don't worry, I'll be here the whole time.
I've wedged the boat into the weeds to keep it in place.
> *The head disappears back down behind the weeds and the wait begins
> again.*

There is a sudden fake bird call from the weeds. Lilly quickly takes her 'staged position again'. She holds this for an uncomfortable amount of time as rustling is heard. This is followed by the sound effects of a group of ducks flying above.

VIOLET: *(continues. She's behind the weeds)* False alarm.

LILLY: I know. Just ducks. Again. *(pause)* Mother, please.
   Violet ignores her

LILLY: *(continues)* We've been here for nearly three hours. *(pause)* I know you can hear me. *(pause)* This whole time all we've seen are three flocks of ducks, a group of school children and a passing mail carriage. Mother! *(pause, then standing)*

VIOLET: Lilly! What on earth are you doing? Sit down immediately!

LILLY: Give me back my oar and then I will sit down.

VIOLET: No!

LILLY: Fine. *(Lilly tries to move the boat forward.)*

VIOLET: What are you doing?

LILLY: Getting out of here one way or another.
   She removes her bonnet, rolls up her sleeves and tries again to move forward.

VIOLET: Don't you dare! Now put that bonnet back on now!

LILLY: No.

VIOLET: You put that back on or...or I'll send you off to your grandmother's for a month.

   Lilly suddenly stops.

LILLY: You wouldn't dare?

VIOLET: Oh yes, I would. In fact, let's make it two months. I'm sure by the end of that time she will have your engagement to Lord Buckmere well and truly confirmed.

LILLY: No, Mother. Please! He comes up to my chin.

VIOLET: He has a title.

LILLY: He also has bad breath, wandering hands and talks more about himself that anyone I have ever met.

VIOLET: Yes, well, if you won't help yourself …..

LILLY: I am trying.

VIOLET: Really? (*She looks at the bonnet on the floor of the boat.*)

LILLY: Kind of.

VIOLET: Darling, I know this is not ideal, but desperate times and all that...

LILLY: Desperate? I've only just turned nineteen.

VIOLET: Don't I know it! This month alone I have received invitations to six of your friends' weddings - five of whom are younger than you.

LILLY: Grace is twenty two and she's still not married.

VIOLET: Yes, and look at her poor mother. She hasn't slept with worry for three years. How old would you say she is?

LILLY: I don't know. Fifty five?

VIOLET: She is forty two. Is that how you want me to look? Is it?

LILLY: Of course not.

VIOLET: Good. Now move closer and I'll help fix your hair and bonnet.
    She stays seated where she is.

LILLY: But no one's coming.

VIOLET: Your Aunt Edith assured me that the hunting party was going boating this afternoon. A hunting party full of very eligible, very handsome, and extremely rich bachelors! We just have to wait a little longer.

LILLY: And if they do happen to arrive? You still haven't even told me what to say, other than, 'Whoops; I've dropped my oar'. Do I allow them to come aboard to rescue me?

VIOLET: Good gracious no!

LILLY: Oh, so you want me to climb on board with a bunch of men fresh from hunting.

VIOLET: Don't be crass! I taught you better than that.

LILLY: Yes you did. And then you threw me in a boat in the middle of nowhere and took away my oar!

VIOLET: I placed you, I did not throw you. And we are not in the middle of nowhere. You can see the Manor if you look through those trees. When they come near, as I told you before, all you need to do is pull that ribbon.

LILLY: Pull it off and wave it around like a flare?

VIOLET: Yes dear, something like that.

   Pause.

LILLY: Can't we just go home?

VIOLET: No. Another hour.

LILLY: An <u>hour</u>?

VIOLET: (*trying a different tactic*) If you stop your complaining, I'll ask cook to prepare something special.

LILLY: I'm not ten years' old, Mother.

VIOLET: Well, if you don't want her famous blueberry crumble and custard, then I guess I won't ask her.

LILLY: (*pause*) Fine. One hour - no more.

VIOLET: Good girl. Now lean over so I can fix up your hair and bonnet. (*Violet leans over the water weeds to fix Lilly's hair.*) You've always had such lovely hair, you know. Ever since you were a child. You get that from my side of the family. And that tiny waist of yours - so perfect for a wedding dress. That you most certainly don't get from me. The more you eat the smaller you seems to get. (*Pause*) You know, your grandmother stopped me eating cake when I was 16. She wanted to ensure my corset would still do up each day.

LILLY: Really?

VIOLET: Oh yes. She told cook she would fire her on the spot if she saw her sneak me anything sweet.

LILLY: But that's cruel!

VIOLET: That's not how she saw it. As far as she was concerned, she was setting me up for the best match possible. (*Pause*) Which is exactly what I'm trying to do for you.

LILLY: But a life of no cake....

VIOLET: I met your father didn't I?

LILLY: Yes... I suppose you did.

VIOLET: There you go. All done. It barely looks like you've had a tantrum. (*pause*) Now, I'm ducking down back here again. Just remember, if you hear the call, pull the ribbon. Don't wait for the boat anymore, just pull it on my call. We're running out of time. (*Violet prepares to duck down.*) I love you, darling.

LILLY: (*reluctantly*) I love you, too.

VIOLET: Good. Now sit up straight.

> *Violet ducks down and disappears behind the weeds. After a short*
> *while the bird calls unexpectedly start.*

LILLY: What!? Oh! (*The bird calls continue.*) Oh dear! (*she flusters to find and pull the ribbon. It is quite stuck so she has to tug it with both hands.*) Mother, it's stuck! It won't pull -

It finally releases and flies into the air and out of the boat. It is the drain plug. Water immediately starts filling inside the boat, shocking Lilly. At the same time, Violet sticks her head up and frantically calls out.

VIOLET: False Alarm! False Alarm! Do not pull the ribbon! Do not pull the ….. Oh Lilly! What have you done?

LILLY: What have I done?! I pulled the ribbon exactly as you said. Now water is pouring in!

VIOLET: Quick put the plug back in!

LILLY: The what?

VIOLET: The plug. They thing you pulled out with the ribbons on it.

LILLY: It flew into the water and now I can't see it!

Violet leans over trying to calm her.

VIOLET: Just try to stay calm. It's just a little bit of water.

LILLY: I can't swim! Help me, Mummy!

VIOLET: You need to find the plug. Quickly! Search in the water.

LILLY: I can't. I'm too scared.

VIOLET: Just search, darling!

LILLY: But what if I fall in?

VIOLET: You won't fall.

LILLY: Or there could be eels!

VIOLET: (*losing control*) Just find the damn plug!

A shocked Lilly searches around her, finally finding the plug.

LILLY: I've found it! I've found it!

VIOLET: Good. Now put it straight back in.

*Lilly manages to replace the plug and the water stops. She drops
down in relief.*

LILLY: I don't understand...I just grabbed the ribbon and... (*realisation dawns
on her*) Oh <u>my God</u>! You tried to kill me!

VIOLET: Oh settle down. I am not trying to kill you. I am just trying to get you
married.

LILLY: But I can't swim. I would have drowned.

VIOLET: No. Your future husband would have dived into save you. And we
would all live happily ever after.

LILLY: Then where is he?

VIOLET: It was a false alarm.

LILLY: No kidding!

VIOLET: Don't take that tone with me.

LILLY: You nearly caused me to drown!

VIOLET: I am still your mother.

LILLY: Barely.

VIOLET: Oh stop being dramatic! The water is only waist deep.

LILLY: What!?

VIOLET: The water only goes up to the waist in this part.

LILLY: Oh. Well...I don't care! I'm never talking to you ever again. In fact, I'd
rather you sent me to Grandmother's. At least she doesn't try to kill her own
daughter!

VIOLET: Yes. Well her daughter married early, didn't she. I didn't make her
worry the way you have me.

LILLY: I didn't get sick on purpose.

VIOLET: Didn't you? You probably did it just to spite me!

LILLY: And maybe you're trying to kill me just to get me back!

They are suddenly interrupted by shouts.

PETER: *(offstage)* Hello there.

VIOLET: What on earth..... ?

PETER: *(offstage)* Is everything okay over there?

LILLY: Mother! It's the hunting party!

VIOLET: Quick, Lilly. Sit up straight! Fix up your hair! Shout for help!

LILLY: *(shouting back offstage, 'Damsel in Distress' voice)* Oh my! Thank goodness someone arrived. I seem to have a leak in my boat. I nearly drowned! I was so afraid; these waters can be so treacherous.

PETER: *(offstage)* Don't panic, we're coming to save you.

VIOLET: Good girl.

LILLY: Mother, do you know who that was? Lord Jamieson's son, Peter!

VIOLET: Oh yes, dear. I know. Quick, lie down and look like you need rescuing!

LILLY: Like this?

VIOLET: Perfect. I'm going to hide.

LILLY: *(pause)* Mother, I'm sorry. I should never have doubted you.

VIOLET: It's okay, dear. *(pause)* A spring wedding would be nice. What do you think?

LILLY: Lovely.

Lilly poses in wait of being rescued as a smug Violet hides again behind the weeds. Sounds of an oncoming row boat, mixed with wedding bells, can be heard as the lights dim.

THE END

A COLODRAMA

by Mike Carter

SYNOPSIS

An old-time Melodrama full of colourful characters and ridiculous verse.

CHARACTERS

SIR BLACK JACK: Aged 50, a middle-aged, debonair cad and bounder.
EARL GREY: Aged 70 ish, a bumbling, ageing aristocrat.
MISS WHITE: Aged 40, a humble but honest governess.
JEAN: Aged 20-25, the flirty daughter of Earl and Countess Grey.
FRED: Handsome 30ish.
LADY SUSAN GREY: Aged 60ish. Haughtily aristocratic.

SETTING

The lounge of a run-down baronial castle in England. A settee is across the corner down left Entrance mid left.

HAND PROPS

A pack of cards, glasses and decanter on table; Miss White's bag behind sofa. Sir Jack has a credit card and a concealed pistol; Fred has a matchbox; Earl Grey has bunch of keys; Lady Susan carries a machine-gun.

Sir Jack and Earl Grey are seated at a card table centre right. Miss White crouches unseen behind the settee.

Sir Jack lays down a card and looks triumphantly at Earl Grey

JACK: So, Earl Grey, not your day. Methinks it is time you repaid your not so inconsiderable debts.

GREY: Alack, Sir Jack, you know the state of my finances. My balance sheet is in the red. You must give me yet a further chance to restore my fortunes. Have pity on me. My wife, the Lady Susan, is in a decline. She has not emerged from her bedroom these past four years. My daughter spends her days reading religious tracts. I've even lost my credit card.

JACK (Aside): I stole it from him yesterday. (Turns to Grey) There still exist your gigantic family jewels. They are worth a fortune.

GREY: The Earl's pearls. (Stands) But no, they are a family heirloom owned by the eldest Grey since the days of William of Orange. Whoever sells them will bring great misfortune upon himself and the family. No, anything but that.

JACK: You have a daughter, Jean whom I find attractive. Give me her hand and I will absolve you of all debts. We will retire to my vast domain in Spain.

GREY: Jean. No, no, she is so innocent, so green in the ways of the world. Poor, poor green Jean. She is too young for you.

JACK: I am determined. *(Rises)* It is she, or the jewels, or bankruptcy.

GREY: Heartless monster. You would take my only child. No wonder they call you, Black Jack.

JACK: Choose.

GREY: It will have to be my daughter.

JACK: Your daughter it is. My queen - Jean.

GREY: Promise you won't be mean to poor green, Queen Jean.

JACK: Curse, the verse gets worse. Go and prepare her for marriage. (*Exit Grey*). Little does the poor fool know we played with my own marked pack. But what is this? A servant girl? …. were you listening?

Miss White emerges from behind couch

WHITE: It is I, Miss White the governess, no serving wench. I was looking for an earring I dropped.

JACK: But you must have been in this room for at least an hour.

WHITE: It was a small earring. But I have good hearing. I heard you confess, Sir Jack, to a stacked pack. I must tell Earl Grey. He is a good, good man. *(Aside)* If only he returned my affection. But alas he is married to that wimp of a wife.

JACK: But your proof? It is your word against mine.

WHITE: And whom, do you think, he will believe? Will it be Black Jack or Lilly White? (*Exits*).

JACK: Dash and blast. I must discredit the woman. I know, I will place this credit card in her handbag which she has most fortuitously left behind the couch. (*Peers over couch*). I knew it. There. (*Picks it up and, places card within. Puts handbag on table*).

Enter Grey, White and Jean.

GREY: I was fetching poor green Jean when Miss Lilly White told me the most incredible story. Could it be, Sir Jack, that you stacked the pack?

JACK: What! Would you believe this woman rather than me? At this very moment, if you investigated the contents of her handbag, I suspect you would find property not belonging to her. Check it for yourself. (*Points to handbag*).

WHITE: That is my bag.

JACK: Come, Lord Grey. Look within.

GREY: Dash it all – a lady's handbag? I cannot.

JACK: Let me shake out the contents. (*Does so*). As I suspected. See!

GREY: My credit card!

WHITE: The bag is mine but I don't know how…

GREY: To believe I trusted you. To believe I let you lull my only daughter to sleep with that wonderful song, Lilly the Pink. Though it breaks my heart to say it, go and never whiten our doorsteps again.

WHITE: Sir!

JACK: You heard your master. Go, faster. (*White exits in tears*). (*Aside*).That was close, blast her. And now. . . green Jean?

GREY: Ah yes, must pop along and see the gardener. The bluebells aren't ringing as they should. I'll leave you two love birds alone. *Exits.*

JACK: Well now. . .a kiss. (*Advances*).

JEAN: No, no .. (*Retreats*).

JACK: Yes, yes. (*Advances*).

JEAN: No, no.. .(*Retreats*).

JACK: I'm, too old for this, dash it. Be sensible.

51

JEAN: No, I cannot marry you. I am betrothed to Fred.

JACK: Who is Fred?

JEAN: He worked here for Daddy four years ago.

JACK: I remember him. A clumsy oaf always getting under people's feet.

WHITE: Yes, an under-footman. He swore he would find a fortune overseas.

JACK: As I recall, his hair was of a carroty shade.

JEAN: Yes, we called him, Fred the Red.

JACK: But Fred the Red fled. He won't return. He's probably a dead Fred. Marry me. I have a vast domain in Spain.

JEAN: A vast domain in Spain?

JCK: I'll say it again. I have …

JEAN: No need. You have made a compelling case. Sir Black I will marry you.

> *Enter Fred.*

FRED: It is I, Fred. I return to claim my betrothed. For the past four years I have milked cows. I have learnt well. (*Turning to Jean*). We can return, buy a herd, get up each morning at five and milk the cows. It will be a hard life, but we will be together.

JEAN: (*Hesitantly*). It sounds…..what can I say…?

FRED: After sixty years we could have our own farm.

> *Enter Grey*

GREY: Good heavens! It's Ted.

FRED: Not Ted, but Fred. I have returned to seek your consent to marry your daughter.

GREY: Sorry old chap, you're too late. I've promised her to Sir Jack.

FRED: Not Black Jack!

GREY: That's what I said, Fred.

JACK: We're to be wed, Fred.

JEAN: You lost by a head, Fred. Actually, Black Jack has a vast domain in Spain.

FRED: (*To Grey*). Sir, the man is a villain. I was talking to my sister Lilly White whom I saw crying on the doorstep. She told me her version of the affair with the credit card. And I can prove it.

JACK: How?

FRED: I have here a portable machine combining DNA profiling with the latest in finger printing technology all bundled together in this matchbox. (*Holds up box*). It was loaned to me by an agent of the CIA who was checking out the New Zealand Government.

GREY: What was his name?

FRED: Agent Lemon. Firstly I will install Black Jack's finger prints taken from the glass he was holding – this is yours*? (Grabs glass from table)*.

JACK: Find out for yourself.

GREY: It was his.

FRED: Now let me examine the credit card. I suspect we will find Black Jack's marks upon it. If there are, we will hear a ting-a-ling ring. (*Bell chimes*).Sort of. Just as I thought. Now I'm going to whack Black Jack.

JACK: No, no, have mercy.

FRED: As I suspected. The fellow's yellow.

JACK: Curses, I am undone.

GREY: Then turn round my dear chap and do yourself up again.

JACK: Yes. I am a villain, but before I go I will have the Earl's pearls. Undo the safe or you die. (*Takes gun from pocket*).

GREY: But if the pearls disappear, misfortune is near.

JACK: Ha ha, away with the house of Grey.

GREY: You bounder. Here, take the keys; the pearls are in the safe. *(Throws over keys)*.

JACK: At last. . (*Unlocks safe and removes pearls*). We will now fly to Spain. Come Jean.

JEAN: Sorry Daddy, good bye Freddie. He has a vast domain in Spain you know…Mummy!

   Lady Susan enters with machine gun.

GREY: Good Heaven's, it's my wife, the Lady Susan. What are you doing down here?

SUE: My gun trumps your gun, methinks, Black Jack. Put it down. (*Jack does so*). Place the pearls on the table and leave this house. And take that dreadful girl with you.

JACK: Dash my teeth. What's happening? (*Puts down pearls*)

JEAN: Yes, Mother, why?

SUE: 'Tis a long involved story. I love Fred

FRED: And I always wanted to woo you, too, Sue. But you were true to your husband.

SUE: No longer. He is enamoured of your sister. They go shopping together. I have seen them.

GREY: You have been so blue, Sue. I needed sunshine and light, I needed Miss White

WHITE: Oh Earl Grey, what can I say?

JACK: (*To Jean*). Let's go. I'm beginning to hate poetry.

JEAN: Now tell me again about your domain in Spain… (*Exeunt*)

GREY: Come my dear, to Marks and Sparks. (*Offers arm to WHITE*).

WHITE: Don't forget the card. (*Grey waves it at her*). Darling. (*Exeunt*)

FRED: That leaves me and you, Sue. What'll we do?

SUE: We'll flog the Earl's pearls and then…

FRED: Yes?

SUE: We'll paint the town red, Fred. (*They skip out hand in hand, Sue brandishing machine gun.*)

THE END

NO LINGERING ALLOWED
a tragicomedy

by Elspeth Tilley

SYNOPSIS
Sometimes thinking about death can help us figure out what it means to live.

CHARACTERS

ADELAIDE: A woman in her 70s.

BERNADETTE: Adelaide's older sister, now retired after a successful career in broadcasting.

GEMMA: Adelaide's room-mate at the palliative care hospice. A very elderly, wizened yet sprightly woman.

SUSAN: A nurse, in her 20s, with a thin build. Starched, efficient and just a tad mean.

SETTING

A hospice room. There are two beds with bedside cabinets, and a window with closed curtains. Some flowers and colourful crochet rugs can't hide the fact that it sounds and looks like a hospital.

HAND PROPS

Two cell phones and a book. An intravenous drip unit on wheels. A bowl of porridge on a hospital tray.

Gemma and Adelaide are asleep in twin beds in a shared hospice room. A cell phone rings. Adelaide picks it up, looks at it, puts it back down again, still ringing, and puts a pillow over her head. Gemma sits bolt upright, suddenly alert.

GEMMA: Are you going to answer that?

ADELAIDE: No.

GEMMA: Maybe you could turn the ringer down a bit, then? (*Aside.*) It's enough to wake the dead.

ADELAIDE: I don't know how. Ridiculous new-fangled thing – I didn't even want it. It's the kids: always giving me things I don't want. (*Coughs.*)

GEMMA: Pass it here.

Gemma fiddles with phone, ring volume decreases then stops, she passes it back.

ADELAIDE: Thank you.

GEMMA: I'm Gemma.

ADELAIDE: Adelaide.

GEMMA: What're you in for?

ADELAIDE: You make it sound like prison.

GEMMA: It kind-of is. We're never going to leave. Except in a box. (*Gemma cackles at herself.*) Anyway, what're you in for?

ADELAIDE: Inquisitive, aren't you?

GEMMA: Me, I'm liver failure. Only myself to blame! Too much of the good life! Mercifully quick though – ten weeks from diagnosis to croak! No lingering allowed! (*Aside.*) Mind you, I never was one for doing what I'm told.

ADELAIDE: You seem chipper about it.

GEMMA: No point moping. I've had a good life. Some times to remember. And now it is what it is. You?

ADELAIDE: The big C.

GEMMA: Oooh, which bit of you?

ADELAIDE: Most of me at this point.

GEMMA: Ah, the lace tablecloth effect – knots and holes all over.

ADELAIDE: I suppose you could say that.

GEMMA: How long have you got?

ADELAIDE: They said maybe a few weeks.

GEMMA: Well, that's good. If it's really dire, they tell you 'one week'. That's their code for 'walking dead.' If they haven't said 'one week', you're all good.

ADELAIDE: I don't see how anything could possibly be good at this point.

GEMMA: Time to sort things out, you know. Mend your bridges. Declare your ceasefires.

ADELAIDE: I have nothing to sort out.

GEMMA: You don't? That ringing phone just now says different to me. (*Adelaide puts the pillow back over her head. Gemma rolls her eyes at the audience.*) Suit yourself.

Susan enters, wheeling an IV stand, and talks to Adelaide.

SUSAN: Awake are we? Let's get some intravenous into you before the oral wears off.

ADELAIDE: Ow!

SUSAN: Hold still. There. Try not to pull it out. Now, shall we open the curtains?

ADELAIDE: No.

Susan opens curtains. Adelaide recoils.

SUSAN: Bit of sunlight will do you good. Some lovely vitamin D. Good for the bones.

ADELAIDE: I hardly think it matters what my bones are doing.

SUSAN: Bone health is very important – you don't want to get osteoporosis.

Susan exits.

ADELAIDE: She's insane.

GEMMA: Bonkers. It helps, for working here.

ADELAIDE: What do I want good bones for, to make a decent pile of ashes at the cremation?

GEMMA: Well, one should always try to look decent.

ADELAIDE: And she's rough. When she put my drip in, it's like she's stabbing her dinner with a bloody great fork. Not that she looks like she eats any dinner. She's like a toothpick.

GEMMA: She should eat a burger. She's so skinny, we'd probably see it going all the way down, like a rat inside a snake. Nurse Toothpick. With lump.

ADELAIDE: She should practise her IV technique. On an orange. That's what we did in my day. There's a lot of resemblance between an orange and the human buttock.

GEMMA: If she was training to do me, she could use a mouldy tomato. Red and wrinkly and growing whiskers in all the wrong places. You've got some medical experience then?

ADELAIDE: No. Not really.

Adelaide picks up a book, ending the conversation. Phone rings, quieter than before but still loud. Adelaide ignores it.

GEMMA: Are you still not answering that?

ADELAIDE: No.

GEMMA: Why not?

ADELAIDE: It's my interfering cow of a sister. She can take a flying leap.

GEMMA: Gosh.

ADELAIDE: I won't be bullied by her.

GEMMA: Good for you.

Phone stops.

ADELAIDE: You'd think when someone's dying, they'd have the right to be left in peace.

GEMMA: Mmm. (*Aside.*) You would.

ADELAIDE: But no. (*Phone rings.*) It's call after call. No rest.

GEMMA: (*Aside.*) No, no rest. (*To Adelaide, sotto voce.*) Look out, it's Nurse Toothpick!

Phone stops ringing. Susan enters with a bowl of porridge on a tray.

SUSAN: Here we are: breakfast. Lovely porridge.

ADELAIDE: I loathe porridge.

SUSAN: Well it's either that or baby food, given the stage you're at. Which would you prefer?

ADELAIDE: I'm not a baby. I still have all my teeth.

SUSAN: Good, then it's porridge for you.

Susan exits.

ADELAIDE: Where's your breakfast?

GEMMA: Oh, I'm long past the eating stage. (*Aside*). Trust me.

ADELAIDE: Lucky you. You're saved from death by grey sludge. You seem alright though. Still full of energy.

GEMMA: It's my last burst. You know, like the final pulse of energy released across the universe from a dying star.

ADELAIDE: That's quite profound. Will it happen to me too?

GEMMA: Depends.

Phone rings.

ADELAIDE: Oh for goodness sake. (*She puts the phone under the bedclothes.*)

GEMMA: What does she want?

ADELAIDE: How would I know?

GEMMA: She's your sister?

ADELAIDE: Mmm. Well, we haven't really spoken for forty-something years. Other than phony 'my condolences dear, my congratulations dear' at funerals and weddings. All such lies.

GEMMA: Really?

Phone stops ringing.

ADELAIDE: She started it.

GEMMA: I see.

ADELAIDE: Well, no, actually, I started the not talking. But she started the thing that started the not talking.

GEMMA: (*Aside, tongue-in-cheek.*) Well, for shame!

ADELAIDE: And now she wants *me* to make *her* feel alright! Can you imagine? I'm the dying one, and she wants to make it all about her.

GEMMA: How's that?

ADELAIDE: I'm guessing she wants her conscience cleared.

GEMMA: What of?

ADELAIDE: Nothing much. Just ruining my life.

GEMMA: Dear me.

ADELAIDE: I would have been a nurse myself if it wasn't for her. But I never graduated.

GEMMA: We could have used you in here. Teach Nurse Toothpick some bedside manner.

ADELAIDE: If she smiled, she might crack.

GEMMA: She'd explode. Shards everywhere. We'd have to wear slippers so as not to get toothpick splinters in our feet. So why aren't you a nurse?

ADELAIDE: I got the sack. For talking to the media. Only I never had. I'd only talked to my sister. As a sister. Not as the media.

GEMMA: She was media?

ADELAIDE: A cadet journalist, back then. Starting out. Looking for her big break. Which she got, thanks to me. Then later, she was really big news. First woman to anchor primetime: Bernadette Walker. She's retired now.

GEMMA: I remember her! She was great! So Bernadette Walker's your sister? Nice.

ADELAIDE: For her.

Susan enters.

SUSAN: Your children are coming. They just rang to check. I said you were fine for visitors and they'll be in at visiting time.

ADELAIDE: I don't want any visitors.

SUSAN: Too late: I told them, three o'clock. And don't be cranky at them. It's difficult for families.

Susan exits.

ADELAIDE: Difficult for *families*? I'm the one with lungs like paper doilies and morphine up the whazoo.

GEMMA: How many you got?

ADELAIDE: Whazoos? Just the one, last time I checked!

GEMMA: (*Giggling.*) No, kids.

ADELAIDE: Two – a boy and a girl. Benjamin, good lad, he's a scientist. Overseas now – but he flew back as soon as he heard they were sticking me in here. The place of no return. And my youngest, she finished her nursing like I should have and travelled right around the world, done her volunteer service abroad, like I would have. (*Coughs.*)

GEMMA: So why didn't you? Travel? Do volunteering?

ADELAIDE: Oh, I've done my share of volunteering. School gala and cake sales 'til I'm blue in the bloody face. But I never finished the nursing training. Got the sack, like I said. Thanks to brilliant Bernadette. I told her some things that were going on at the hospital where I was training. Things I didn't agree with. Just getting it off my chest, you know. I never thought it would go anywhere. But she published a big exposé. Patient maltreatment on Ward 19. Front page. Of course they traced it back to me, and I got my marching orders.

GEMMA: Ouch. Tough break. Did you talk to her about it?

ADELAIDE: No need. I was her sister, they knew it came from me. Next thing, I've got no job, rent to pay, and no references.

GEMMA: What did you do?

ADELAIDE: I got a typing job, then I got married quick smart. Wedding, kids, nappies, carpooling. Zero chance of zipping off to Médecins Sans Frontières with all that going on. Mind you, the after-school pickup run was just about a war zone most days.

GEMMA: Still…

ADELAIDE: What?

GEMMA: Well - they sound like great kids. You seem proud of them.

ADELAIDE: Oh not you too. 'Be grateful for what you've got' and all that pious muck? 'Forgive and forget'? If I'm going to die, I want to die the way I lived.

GEMMA: What, pig-headed?

ADELAIDE: No, honest! Call a spade a spade, not pretend everything's been rosy when it hasn't! (*Coughs.*)

GEMMA: Sounds like you haven't got as long as you think.

ADELAIDE: None of your business.

GEMMA: I'm just saying. When it's too late, it's too late. You know, for (*aside*) pious muck.

ADELAIDE: Hmph.

Adelaide's snort turns into a coughing fit. Phone rings. Adelaide picks it up and looks at it. Lights drop to blackout with just a special on Adelaide. She answers the phone.

Hello? (*Beat.*) Yes, Bernie, it's me answering my own phone. Who did you think it would be, Florence bloody Nightingale? God, yes, I suppose so. If you must.

Gemma exits under cover of the blackout, while Adelaide is speaking. When Adelaide finishes her phonecall, lights come up full, and Susan enters with Bernadette.

SUSAN: Visitor time! Your children aren't here yet, but look who I found! Your sister!

Susan exits.

BERNADETTE: Hello Adelaide.

ADELAIDE: Hello Bernadette. (*Coughs.*)

BERNADETTE: Goodness, that sounds bad. Do you want some water?

ADELAIDE: Water doesn't bloody help. I just wanted to talk.

BERNADETTE: I know.

ADELAIDE: I've got some things to say. That's why I answered your call. We should have talked a long time before now.

BERNADETTE: I .....

ADELAIDE: You betrayed my confidence. The one person I trusted, and... (*Coughs.*)

BERNADETTE: For what it's worth, Addy, I know what you're going to say, but it wasn't how you think. I had it from other sources. Multiple people from the hospital had spoken to me well before you did. I couldn't sit on something unethical once I knew about it.

ADELAIDE: What, you knew? When I was agonising over spilling my guts to you, it was already old news to you? Why didn't you say?

BERNADETTE: Because I couldn't. We have to keep confidential what we know. Protect our sources. It's our most fundamental promise, as journalists. But the hospital wouldn't believe me that it wasn't you, if I wouldn't tell them other names. And I couldn't. I protected all my sources, including you.

ADELAIDE: And then I didn't believe you either. All these years. Damn, I was stubborn.

BERNADETTE: I know.

ADELAIDE: Anyway, it's my new friend Gemma we have to thank now. She nagged me into answering the phone. Where's she gone? Nurse?

Susan enters.

SUSAN: Yes?

ADELAIDE: Where's Gemma gone?

SUSAN: Who?

ADELAIDE: Her - the woman in the other bed.

SUSAN: Clearly, I have given you way too much pain med, haven't I? That bed's been vacant for weeks. I'll double check your dose.

Susan exits.

ADELAIDE: She wasn't a hallucination. We were talking.

BERNADETTE: It's alright; it's a common symptom. It's the cancer; it triggers visions. Old memories.

ADELAIDE: She seemed very real.

BERNADETTE: Brain mets can do that. The nurse'll fix your dose. Gosh she's a skinny one. She looks like that girl we used to flat with – do you remember? We nicknamed her The Toothpick.

ADELAIDE: (*Laughing.*) We used to try to get her to eat a burger, 'cause we reckoned we'd see it going all the way down.

BERNADETTE: Oh, God, we were truly awful, weren't we – talk about skinny shaming! We should know better now, at this age.

ADELAIDE: Screw that! Nurse Toothpick is hangry as hell and she needs a feed before she stabs someone half to death with that bloody needle. And you know what? I can say whatever I damn well please now!

BERNADETTE: You can. You definitely can.

ADELAIDE: I should have started doing it earlier. Let's order a pizza for her. And one for us. This porridge is killing me.

Adelaide hides the porridge in her bedside drawer. Bernadette gets out her phone and starts ordering pizza online.

BERNADETTE: Deep dish or thin crust, what do you reckon?

ADELAIDE: Definitely deep dish. With extra cheese.

BERNADETTE: Good. Now, tell me about those gorgeous kids of yours. And how many grandkids? I can't wait to meet them all.

THE END

ABOUT THE AUTHORS

Kerrie Anne Spicer is an Auckland writer who dreams of giving up her day job and writing full time. Her 10 minute plays have been performed in Auckland, Whangarei, Palmerston North, Sydney, Melbourne, and Brisbane. She is currently engrossed in novel writing.

Tim Hambleton is a lawyer, police prosecutor, and playwright from Dunedin. He has written four full length comedies which have been produced by repertory societies around New Zealand. Tim has also written a number of successful 10 minute plays, a one act comedy and penned a script for a school production. He is married with two children.

Richard Prevett is a Matamata accountant who wasted his youth competing in sports events before wandering into amateur theatre and eventually plunging into writing plays, both comedy and drama. All his plays have been performed in Hamilton and/or Matamata.

Dolly Varden-Chambers hails from Essex, England and now lives in 'Hobbiton', Waikato, New Zealand. Dolly is happily both a mother and grandmother. She has considerable theatrical experience as an actor, singer and director. Dolly is also an artist and author. She has published a book of her plays and other works.

Lindsey Brown is a high school teacher of both English and Drama, with a particular passion for performing. She has acted in an array of stage shows including straight plays, musicals and improvisation. In 2017 she studied for a Masters of Scriptwriting at AUT. Now she is, more than ever, eager to write stage plays both for adults and for use in the classroom.

Mike Carter recently moved to live in Tauranga. He is a Life Member of the Onewhero Society of performing Arts where he has variously written, directed, prompted, and forgotten lines in a number of productions. Mike has had short stories published nationally, and broadcast on Radio New Zealand. He enjoys playing music, tramping and writing whatever springs to mind.

Elspeth Tilley is a graduate of the University of Queensland drama programme, and now teaches theatre and creative activism at Massey University Wellington. She is a two-time winner of the British Theatre Challenge and three-time official playwright for Climate Change Theatre Action. Her short plays have been produced worldwide, and published in the USA, UK and Canada.

June Allen: After many years of acting on stage June successfully turned her hand to playwriting. She is a play script assessor for Short+Sweet International Festival. Her very popular children's stories featuring New Zealand and Pacifica wildlife are published by Kwizzel Publishing. June is a Life Member of Playwrights Association of New Zealand.

Email: kwizzelnewzealand@gmail.com
Facebook: Kwizzel Publishing